MVFOL

D1015482

Ten-Second Rainshowers

Ten-Second Rainshowers

POEMS BY YOUNG PEOPLE

COMPILED BY

Sandford Lyne

ILLUSTRATIONS BY

Virginia Halstead

Simon & Schuster Books for Young Readers

The author wishes to thank the many schools, programs, and individuals who made this book possible: Francis Asbury Elementary (Hampton, Va.); University Park Elementary (Hyattsville, Md.); Lynette Baldwin and the Paducah (Ky.) schools; Clark Elementary and the Charlottesville (Va.) schools; Paul Canady and the Richmond (Va.) schools; Anamae Hill and the Henrico County (Va.) schools; Larry Van Nostrand, Betty Smith, Helen Waid, Beverly Flowers, Paula Tortolini, Patsy Garner, Patricia House, and the Virginia Beach (Va.) city schools; the schools of Falls Church, Fairfax County, and Alexandria (Va.); the Arlington Humanities Project (Va.); Kathy Carroll and Scott Montgomery Elementary (Washington, D.C.); Mary Colwell and Caldwell Fine Arts (Idaho); Armstrong Elementary (Hampton, Va.); Trinity Lutheran (Newport News, Va.); St. Mary's and St. Stephen's and St. Agnes (Alexandria, Va.); and Eileen Ford and the Chesterfield County (Va.) schools.

 SIMON & SCHUSTER BOOKS FOR YOUNG READERS

An imprint of Simon & Schuster Children's Publishing Division,
1230 Avenue of the Americas, New York, New York 10020.

Book design by Paul Zakris
The text of this book is set in 13-point Stemple Schneidler.
The illustrations are rendered in oil pastel.
Manufactured in the United States of America
First Edition
10 9 8 7 6 5 4 3 2

Library of Congress Cataloging-in-Publication Data

Ten-second rainshowers : poems by young people / compiled by Sandford Lyne ;
  illustrations by Virginia Halstead.
    p. cm.
Summary: A collection of poems about childhood, family, nature, and other subjects, written by young people ranging in age from eight to eighteen. Includes index.
ISBN 0-689-80113-0
1. School verse, American. 2. Children's writings, American. 3. Teenagers' writings, American. 4. American poetry—20th century. [1. American poetry—Collections.
2. Children's writings. 3. Teenagers' writings.] I. Lyne, Sandford. II. Halstead, Virginia, ill.
PS591.S3T38 1996   95-10710

To the memories of my daughter,
Sara Maud Kidder-Lyne,
and my mother, Evelyn Lyne

Contents

Introduction

Early one summer morning, when I was eight, my father woke me with uncharacteristic softness, almost a whisper. He told me we were going out in the backyard "to hunt for buried treasure." What could he mean? I wondered. My father was many things to me, but not a man of mysteries.

We went out to a place in the backyard near the small, converted barn-garage. There my father put into my hands a small, boy-sized shovel. He stood there silently for a few moments, surveying a scruffy patch of dirt and grass. "This looks like a good spot. Let's try here," he said, and motioned for me to dig. I dug for a few minutes and, sure enough, I found a dime! Excited by my success, I began to dig in another place. After a while, my father said again, "Why not try here?" Again I dug where my father pointed, and this time I found a quarter. This went on for quite some time, me digging in various places and, now and then, my father offering a suggestion: "Try here," or "This looks like it might have something." It was amazing to me how my father seemed to guess all of the places where I'd find a coin.

A few months afterward, a little older (and a little wiser), I asked my father about that "treasure hunt." He told me that while I was busy digging in one place, he'd drop a coin behind me in another place, pressing it into the ground with his foot; the first coin he had buried and marked with a stick. We had a good laugh about this. To this day, I don't know how my father thought of it.

In a very real sense, this book is the result of many successful treasure hunts. "My life is/a buried treasure/to me," third-grader Dawn Withrow writes. "I want/to find it./I dig all day./It is very hard/to find it/all by myself." With dazzling candor and freshness, the young poets in this collection remind us of the pure origins of poetry: the simple human need to record a pain or a joy and to know that one's own words are more than enough.

The title of this book—*Ten-Second Rainshowers*—celebrates these young poets' sudden and complete surrender to inspired awareness, insight, and expression. They get on and off the page quickly—and back to living. Like those small rain clouds that appear as if from nowhere in a sun-filled sky, raining just a few moments and then moving on, leaving behind them a great refreshment upon all things, so do these poems shower for just a few moments on the empty page—and leave for us a renewed sense of the richness, wonder, and purposes of life.

All of the contributors to this book were briefly my students when I worked in their primary or secondary schools as a visiting poet between 1983 and 1994. They came from a variety of racial, ethnic, religious, and socioeconomic backgrounds, and they lived in urban, suburban, and rural areas. All wrote their poems in a short space of time, in the classroom or as a home assignment. Regardless of their backgrounds or educational levels, I found that most needed very few things to start writing: safe and sensible starting places, a few guidelines (for example, don't try to rhyme), and the "fairy dust" of attention and praise. Gathered together, their words represent the complex experience of childhood, evoked not as a remembrance, but rather caught alive in its own true, poetic voice.

Many of the poets in this collection, dipping their hands into the rushing stream of childhood, are startled by how quickly it is running by them, wistful that they are unable to slow its brisk charge ahead. Some simply wish a difficult childhood to be over; others are drawn by a future whose mysterious pull sometimes throws a young life into great confusion and promises something one cannot quite imagine. And still others point to an amazing phenomenon: we live multidimensionally. There is a staircase between this world and the place of our origins, and each step reaches, through experience and awareness, to the other steps both above and below it. The young poets in this anthology often play nimbly up and down the staircase, hinting at their connections to other worlds while emphasizing the need to make the lower part of the staircase, the earthly world, their temporary home. "The creek is my friend" writes seventh-grader Scott Denson, "it talks with me by/falling over the rocks,/but the sun also/likes my friend/and likes to take him/in the sky."

I have now taught poetry writing to over 27,000 young people. It was not a work I consciously planned for, and I marvel constantly at how it came to pass. I often remember back to that special summer morning, digging in the yard with my father. I dug up plenty of other treasures, too, that day—wonderful roots and beautiful stones, insects and grubs and long wriggly worms (which I saved in a can for fishing), an old nail or two. I found three dollars that morning and had the time of my life—and, of course, my father got his garden dug.

A few years into my teaching, I realized that my father's invention was a universal way to reach out to young people. "Try this," I say, introducing an approach to making a poem. "Dig here. Maybe this will have something for you." The treasure found is always more than the treasure buried. The implement used is a soft lead pencil. Everywhere I look, I see the garden.

—Sandford Lyne

As I write
these words most
will likely be
forgotten but it took
time of my life
to do it

—SCOTT DENSON
Grade 7

Angels in Bloom

POEMS ABOUT
CHILDHOOD

*Do you know what the best thing you can do
for this world is? Have a good time.*

—KEN CAREY
from *Notes to My Children*

Masters

We march out of the classroom
like angels in front of the teacher,
but when we get outside onto
the soft earth we run and yell
and fight and scream.
We are no longer angels.
We are masters at childhood.

—JENNIFER EDWARDS
Grade 6

I Feel Awesome

I feel awesome when my friends and I
raid the subway construction.
We crawl on the ground out of sight.
People see it as mischief even though
we don't touch a thing.

—THOMAS WAGNER
Grade 4

Let's go swim in the river.
Then let's climb up the barge
and play in the coal.
Now we're living shadows.

—BRAD WILLIAMS
Grade 6

Thief

I am like a thief.
Sometimes when I want to
go out I will sneak
under the fence. The flowers
will sometimes tell on me.
But sometimes I will
make it to the field.

—ERIN DEVINE
Grade 5

Fall in Fourth

I like to see the leaves fall low. And see
the clouds up high. But most of all I'm glad
I'm still a fourth-grade kid.

—CHRISTOPHER ENGEL
Grade 4

The Dragon

The homework papers
are slow being passed
up, moving like snails.
When the teacher sees
the light load she yells
like a red dragon. Her
voice as well as the
heater keeps us warm.

—KEVIN HALL
Grade 8

One morning our teacher read
a long story.
When it was over, our teacher
looked like a book.

—GEORGINA BRUER
Grade 3

Today Has Been Turned Upside Down

I missed three problems on my
    math paper.
I didn't answer any problems in
    Social Studies.
And outside I see a bare tree
with barely any leaves on it.
I hear the cold, harsh wind blow.
I also see geese fly somewhere where
    it is warmer.
But sitting here writing this poem
around my friends makes me feel good.
And seeing my friends write
    beautiful poems
also makes me feel good.

—ANTHONY JAECKS
Grade 5

Today

Today is a day for fun
No chores
No yard work
Just play
As I play outside
I don't hear anything
Just silence
But tomorrow is another day
Full of chores
Chores surrounding me
Tomorrow there will be work
Lots of it
So I'll have a good time today
And then tomorrow
I'll be ready for work

—KELLY JOHNSON
Grade 5

Freewheeling

On my bike I feel free.
No one knows where I am.
Only I know.
I have no worry
in the world except
the car behind me.

—JOANNE WATTERS
Grade 5

Freedom

The girls stand there over the fountain,
thinking of their freedom to take
off their sandals and swim forever.

—DAVID PRYOR
Grade 9

Never Too Late

Outside I play around
the dogwood tree.
I still have homework,
but I don't have time.
I don't know why my mother
won't write a note.
Only thing she says is,
"It was your job.
Now let it be late."
But my teacher says
it is never too late.

—JENNIFER TAYLOR
Grade 4

Growing Up

We are girls, and we're proud.
We make mistakes when we're
growing—maybe tears, maybe not.
We have dreams because we're girls.

—WENDY GARRETT
Grade 4

The whole class is talking
There's nothing to do
I guess I will sit here and
Bloom

—ADAM COOKE
Grade 3

All Evening

From her rocking chair
the old woman
flung wild tales
across the hearth
at me
I worked hard
to catch them all evening

—ASHLEY MAY
Grade 7

A Pillow

A pillow is everything
to me. I need it under
my head to go
to sleep. My pillow
is everything to me.
I'm writing this poem
and I need my
pillow with me.

—ALICEA MCCOY
Grade 5

Forever and a Day

I want to go home.
The day is long.
It has been long ever since
I woke up.

—HEATHER LACHMAN
Grade 4

Children

Children are like
Precious flowers
That break if you
Don't treat them right.
They were angels
In another world
And hope to become
Human in this world
And also grow like flowers.
That's why nobody should
Be left out.

—JANICE ALFARO
Grade 6

Running

When I am running,
my arms cut through the
breeze like knives. As I am
running through the gate
I say to myself, today, today
is a beautiful day to run.

—JESSE BURKITT
Grade 7

Happy

Happy by myself sitting by a car.
Being alone in the snow sitting by a log.
I feel like an elf,
a peasant who knows nothing.
I am the smallest one around.

—KEVIN HAMMOND
Grade 5

Punishment

The Emperor has punished me
for being wrong.
His men throw mud and rocks.
I scold myself.
It seems my last years
will be full of purple
as I lie in the weeds.

—DANIEL HAVEY
Grade 5

Toad's Song

Every night I lay awake
I hear the toads sing
a special song to me.
They sound beautiful
because you cannot see
their plainness.

—JENNIFER MORRISON
Grade 7

Shortcut

The shortcut takes me through fields
   of flowers,
And past walls of trees where foxes live,
And flitting butterflies.
Past all these things I hurry by.
I ignore all of them, each and every one,
Not so sure I'm glad I took
The shortcut to adulthood.

—ALEX SHANGRAW
Grade 6

My Place

POEMS ABOUT
HOME & FAMILY

*I decided very early to love my family, and to
see in each of its members something rare and
good as well as the miserable and painful
things that were obvious. I do not think that
in writing of them I ever lied. I merely chose
to notice in them the things I cherished and
preferred, and to refer to the things I didn't
cherish with humor and charity.*

—WILLIAM SAROYAN
from *The Bicycle Rider in Beverly Hills*

Warmth

I walked through the empty kitchen
to the door,
to leave the warmth of home
for the bitter-cold anxiety of
a Monday at school.
Ducking the old dogwood outside,
I heard a familiar call,
and turned to see my mother
waving me off to school,
sending me a small fire
to keep my heart a little warmer.

—RICHARD FURST
Grade 10

I Used to Be

I used to be the
only one
till I was two.
One cold night,
the dog lay on
the floor.
The wind blew.
Now I'm the oldest.

—AUTUMN BARNES
Grade 4

Glad to Be Alive

"When you were born,"
my mother said, "you were
a beautiful baby.
I loved to hear you cry. I cried
with you. I was
so glad you were alive.
I didn't know what I would do
without you."

—CAPRICIA QUICK
Grade 4

Claire

That day
was an unusual one.
The warmth came
into my room.
My little sister was lying
beside me
for there was only one bed
for us.
I loved the smell of her,
so sweet
and warm.
She woke up and kissed
me on the jaw.
I really loved her.
I wish I could have
captured that moment
just to make me
feel good inside again.

—MARLENE KENNEY
Grade 5

When Supper's Done

Should I tell the truth?
Or should Mother hear lies?
Lies about the pot roast
Burned to a crisp
Lies about the dryness
I feel at my lips
Lies about things
Said and done
Lies about Father
I don't want to say
Lies I know
Will come out someday
These lies I feel
Burn inside
These lies I feel
Will come out in time

—SADA PARISH
Grade 8

A Gift

I walk down a path
deep into the woods.
I carry a box
wrapped with ribbon.
It is a gift from my mother.
She said not to open it
until I'm alone.
But that will never be,
for as far as I walk
there is a silvery circle
following me.

—KATHERINE POTTER
Grade 6

Traveling

Traveling in the cold night—that's
what my loving father does.
His strong body is cold and shallow.
His soul tells him to go home.

—KENDRA PAGE
Grade 5

Dad and I were not close.
One day he asked me to
go fishing.
I felt this was a way to
make him proud of me.
Grass so green . . .
Dew smelling so sweet . . .
We started out.
My dad caught six while
I caught none.
I felt I had let him down.
My dad must have felt this,
for he took my hand and
told me he was proud
and glad we spent the day
together.

—MARY PATTERSON
Grade 8

Before Bedtime

Lying,
with my pillow tucked
Neatly under my head,
Reading
A book with
Mysteries,
Fairy tales,
Enjoying it
More and more.
Then,
Like a silent butterfly
Moving among the
Grasses,
My mother
Kisses me on my
Oval face.

—PHILLIP KIRLIN
Grade 6

Water

Once when I was in Kentucky
visiting my grandparents, my
granddad asked for some water.
At first I was scared because
of the long walk I had
to the house. I filled a jug
with water the fountain bore and
ran quickly to my grandfather's
despair. When he finally drank
it, he said pleasedly that
his thirst had been quenched,
and I got the water quickly.

—Lance Hansen
Grade 8

Grandfather

My grandfather,
the needle thinness
in him shows.
He stands in the
shadows of the sun.
I cannot place my
grandfather gone.
My grandfather
cannot leave me.
He is mine.
He is all I have.

—LIZ MCDOUGAL
Grade 6

On a Texas Road

I remember on a Texas road
there was construction up ahead;
the road was too narrow for our
    mobile home.
We hit a pole and went across a ditch
into a farmer's field.
My baby brother was laughing;
my mom was screaming as if in pain.
A man came out to see if we were okay.
The wheat in the farmer's field was
    glowing
in the sunset. It was all over just like that.

—DONALD KREHELY
Grade 8

Forget Eden

Yesterday,
my mother stood barefoot in the grass,
hanging clothes out to dry.
She sang,
stretching her spirit out
to meet the distant fire of the noonday sun.
Behind her,
a meaningless snake slithered
through the sheets.
My mother turned around,
and sang to him.

—ANDY WOODFIN
Grade 11

Encouragement

Summer nights
My mom
Finds the love
We need

—TIM McINTOSH
Grade 9

In Dedication to My Loving Mother

When I go to help my mother
   on Saturday
I see her soft hands touch the rough
   floor. I
don't say anything but deep in my
   heart I know
how much she has suffered over the years
   and I tell
her that I love her; but that is not enough
   to pay
what she has given me. Not all the money
   in the world
could fill such a deep hole of hard work
   and depression
of pure suffering, suffering that she does
   not deserve;
but she tells me that that payment can be
   paid
just by working hard in school and
   making her happy;
that way everything can be repaid.

—JOSÉ MACATO
Grade 7

The boy wishes
forgiveness from
his father. He
cries in the night.
He feels a need.
At last,
his father comes in.
His father gives his
forgiveness. But
the boy still feels
a need for love.

—JENNIFER WALLACE
Grade 8

A strange man knocked on the door;
my mother opened it and began to cry.
I didn't know why she cried,
but I cried too!

—ROD ANNET
Grade 12

Mom's Way

There is a clothesline
in my yard.
My mom goes there
every day.
She can't stay away.
There is a reason
every time
at sundown she is
out there still.

—Emma Wadsworth
Grade 4

I am so proud of my father.
I saw my father
in the garden.
I saw my father
holding a hoe.
I saw my father
covered with dust,
which is why
I am so proud of my father.

—Miguel Herrero
Grade 5

The Way Home

On the way home from school,
a light breeze crosses my face.
As I pass the bridge
I can see beautiful horses
grazing in the meadow.
And then the silence of my shadow
meets the door of home.

—AMANDA KELLER
Grade 5

Black
& Blue

POEMS ABOUT
CHALLENGES

The lost child cries, but still he catches fireflies.

—RYUSUI YOSHIDA

Windy Heart

What will happen if the wind
    blows and blows?
I wonder what I'll do
    if the wind blows again
and the light of my heart
    turns black and blue.

—JOEY BENNETT FLOWERS
Grade 6

Left Out

I feel left out today. I guess I'm a nobody.
I guess I'm a piece of leftover pea pod.
I'll walk along the beach and think while
    skipping stones forever.

—CAROLINE HUMPHREY
Grade 3

Wonder to My Eyes

I wonder if I could
be what I want to be.
I wonder if I could
be as wonderful as I want.
I wonder if the world
won't pick on me anymore.
I just want to be
wonderful to my eyes.

—JILL SOUTIERE
Grade 5

Mad

I feel mad when my little brother
    knocks over a chair and pulls
    the tablecloth down, just for
    the fun of it,
when I leave my shoes outside
    in a storm, and they get
    soaking wet,
also when the little elf digs a
    hole in the kitchen floor,
    a pit,
and when my parents wake me
    up when I'm deeply
    asleep.

—BETH TOSSELL
Grade 4

I see a young boy
Saying he's going to run away.
Deep inside,
It's already happened.

—RONNY DIBBERN
Grade 8

In my bed
with covers over my nose
I feel my warmth vibrating
back to me.
This is the love I am so willing
to give, but have no one
to take it.

—CROCKETT KIDWELL
Grade 7

The Day My Mom Went Away

I was in the 9th grade when my mom passed away. I remember it snowed all that day. It was a very pretty snow. The doctor came into the hall where my family stood as we watched the snow slowly drift down onto the ground, and he said we could go in to see her. When I went into the room and held my mother's hand, she acted as though nothing was wrong and told me to take care of everyone; at that time her eyes closed and her warm hand clinched mine. I am glad she got to see all her kids, and got to see the snow. When I walked out of the room, one of my nephews who was five years old at the time looked up and said, "Maybe God needed a good sewer!" Maybe he was right, who knows; my mother was a seamstress.

—Tim Sonderson
Grade 12

A Death in the Family

My cousin has died,
she was my best friend.
I hide my tears
with a walk in the woods.
My cousin has died,
she was my best friend.

—ANNIE RABENHORST
Grade 5

When My Mom Died

When my mom died
I was like the winter
With only a young pine growing
Just the pine and a stump of a great poem

—JAMES POWELL
Grade 8

Mirrors

I look in the mirrors; I see;
I like; but when people see
what I have grown to like
they tease me till
my heart has stopped.

—ERIN MCRAE
Grade 8

Bullied

As I wait at the bus stop,
my heart feels like stone.
My spirit is out of me
as a bully makes fun of me.
I have no energy to fight back,
but his work to put me down
will never be complete.

—JAMES SWETNAM
Grade 4

My Friend

I remember a girl
named Jeanine.
She was one of my friends.
One day at school,
they told us she had cancer.
A week later they said
she was dead.
She's like a plant that
I forgot to water.

—JESSICA SURRAT
Grade 6

Sadness

I was sad one day because
my bird died. It was a
sad day, but it did not
spoil my day. Voices in
my ear sounded like a
bird chirping away. That
is the way of sadness.

—HASHIEM PITTMAN
Grade 6

To Tell a Lie

The day is gloomy.
I'm slow to get out of bed.
I don't feel like going to school.
My mother is yelling.
The yard is muddy.
The bus is late.
So this is what it feels like to tell a lie.

—SCOTT LEIGH
Grade 7

Life

I sit here
all by myself
slowly dying
with fading health,
not because I am
sick or ill,
but because
my life's so still.

—TROY CAMPBELL
Grade 7

I am an ugly little girl.
I am so ugly
   my shadow
      doesn't want to follow me.
        It just runs away.
I am full of joy when I lie in the field
   of violets by the river.
You, violets, are the only ones who
   don't care
   how I look. You only think of what's
in my heart.

—JINA COOPER
Grade 6

Betrayed

When I was only eight years old,
My father left and never came back.
I had sorrow in my eyes for several years.
The blackbirds that I had seen
Reminded me of him—
Even though I did not want to know—
And they were sitting in my backyard.

—ALBERT DRUMMOND
Grade 5

My heart goes out
to the one flower lying dead in
the center of
a soccer field.

—FAITH DUBUC BLANTON
Grade 11

Saying Good-bye

I said good-bye to the praying mantis
    that had been sitting at my window.
I said good-bye to the soft breeze that
    had kept me cool in the hot weather.
I said good-bye to the windowsill as I
    moved away from it.
I said good-bye to the old torn pillow as
    my mother threw it away.
I said good-bye to all these things as I
    prepared to move.

—THEIA WASHINGTON
Grade 4

Concern

What deeds has the universe forgotten?
I try to feel the message.
And my ears find the shameful mistakes.

—CHRIS FUSCO
Grade 8

My Life Is A Buried Treasure

My life is
a buried treasure
to me. I want
to find it.
I dig all day.
It is very hard
to find it
all by myself.

—DAWN WITHROW
Grade 3

Words for You

I am here under a tree,
missing you
and all known others.
Do you know I want to go back,
send my eyes to every street?
Do you know I long to speak
our own beautiful language?
I only wish I am a poet,
to write about you and write for you.
Do you know even in my sleep
I have your name, the most poetic city?
(That is Huế City with Húóng
River and Núingú Mountain,
very tender and special.)

—VUI TRAN
Grade 12

The Door of Stone

A leaf falls, and a door opens
That is made of stone.

—SARA KIDDER-LYNE (1972–1990)
Grade 6

POEMS ABOUT
NATURE & BEAUTY

Through that forest I can pass
Till, as in a looking-glass,
Humming fly and daisy tree
And my tiny self I see. . . .

—Robert Louis Stevenson
from *A Child's Garden of Verses*

Nature

What wonderful things
that nature put on this earth
butterflies and flamingos
but the best is the river

—JARED JACKSON
Grade 7

Lazy Days

With my fishing I sink my problems.
With my hook I catch my joys.
This is the calmness that you search
tirelessly for.
No clock is here to count your time,
no persons to disturb you,
just a fishing pole and a riverbank,
watching away my fears.

—MATT WHITE
Grade 7

Walking through the Woods

I was walking in the woods
When the woods started walking with me.
I love walking with the woods,
and the woods love walking with me.

—DWAYNE FISHER
Grade 7

It is deer season
and you go in the woods.
You sit like a tree
until a deer comes, then you're a leaf
that has been blown by a mysterious wind.

—BRYAN DEWELL
Grade 8

The Wind

What is the wind?
Well, the wind blows.
You can feel it on your nose.
You can feel it on your face.
In fact you can feel it
In any place.
I know if you could see it
It would be beautiful.
I'm so sure if it could show it
It would be merciful.

—LANCE SCHONE
Grade 5

The Beauty of My Mom and Cats

Some beauty of mine
runs through
my mother, my cats.
When the beauty shows,
it's wondrous to feel
the love
in my mom and cats.

—WILLIAM GREENWOOD
Grade 7

My violin's soft music
makes me feel relaxed.
It's like traveling in my dad's truck
from busy Virginia to flat, warm Kansas.

—TONDRA SEIBRING
Grade 8

Trees in the Wind

As I look
I see outside
some trees
some are dead
some are not
When they blow
they look like
they are writing
in the sky

—LAURA DODSON
Grade 7

I see a tree
planted for beauty
by an unbeautiful thing.
It certainly helps
for all that I know.

—CHRISTIAN NORRIS
Grade 5

The Tractor

Inside the old, red barn
near the half-empty rack of hay
where the sunlight filters through
a widening crack,
the beauty of the tractor
catches my eye.

—ALEC HATHAWAY
Grade 6

Beginning of Fall

Our beautiful sky darkens for fall.
My heart jumps out to the falling leaves.
But at least they die in their best look.

—SUMMER HUGHES
Grade 6

The birds are not chirping
Everything is silent
except the sound
of the wind
whistling through my ears
There is no sun
to be seen
only clouds
This day is like
a birdcage
with a cover over it.

—MIKE SAWYER
Grade 8

An April Day

Here I am in April
when the trees and grass
are both green. I'm sitting
here in the shade with dirt.
When I enjoy nature I hear
voices in my head.

—PETER MAGIELNICKI
Grade 4

It was Christmas and it began to snow.
My mom told me to watch for geese.
But all I saw was a big frozen cauliflower
    in the garden.

—JOE LILLER
Grade 8

The cow lay basking in the sun
as nearby flowers swayed.
A mouse scuttled by
in search of a little something to eat.
Each spoke to the field
without saying a word.

—IVANA PERKINSON
Grade 8

The sky is beautiful, like a flower.
The leaves are blowing in the deep
    breeze.
The coins in my pocket are like bells.
My heart is beating slowly.

—RYAN BAHAM
Grade 4

Today the sun shines
down hard, making it warm
but chilly, with the cool
breeze that comes from
nowhere; at this time of
the year, spring and
winter fight for custody
of the season.

—MATT MILLER
Grade 10

The wind I can't see
but I feel and hear
and it must be a spirit
for when it passes
I see trees
bow down to worship.

—NELLO CARAMAT
Grade 5

The Beauty of the Night

Beauty does not bless those
    with freckles on their nose.
I'm no exception to the rule.
But at sundown the sky transforms
    into the darkest shadow.
Under it I hide and the world can't see.
With the night on my nose
    I possess beauty.

—JENNIFER SADLER
Grade 11

As I pass by,
the flowers sing to me.
Their petals glisten in the sunlight;
their colors fill me up,
as I pass by.

—JOE BRIGGS
Grade 10

The Pathway

I see a long path
in the dark woods.
If I go on it
all the leaves
on the trees
will fall on me.

—JOHN LIPFERT
Grade 4

Let's walk together
and not apart
and see what the beauty
really is.

—TREVA WILSON
Grade 6

What I Saw

I sat down by the water and this is what I saw: a beautiful fish, blue and gold. It was stranded in between two rocks and was scared to death. I picked it carefully up and set it down into the water deep enough to swim. It rushed quickly away. Then it came back and blew a bubble at me and left, never to be seen by my eyes again.

—LEIGH DEVLIN
Grade 7

Rainshowers

Rainshowers
last forever, seconds
at a time, and
almost like a poem
which is long
at heart.

—MIKE DAVIS
Grade 8

Holding Hands

POEMS ABOUT
FRIENDSHIP & LOVE

*"Real isn't how you are made," said the
Skin Horse. "It's a thing that happens to you.
When a child loves you for a long, long time,
not just to play with, but REALLY loves you,
then you become Real."*

"Does it hurt?" asked the Rabbit.

*"Sometimes," said the Skin Horse, for he
was always truthful. "When you are Real you
don't mind being hurt."*

—MARGERY WILLIAMS
from *The Velveteen Rabbit*

What Parents Don't Know

My parents don't know
all the girls that are kissed by boys
The ladders of the tree house
come down to them

—OLIVIA BERGQUIST
Grade 4

Lazy Days

My lazy days I'm at the creek,
standing alone upon my favorite log,
thinking, wishing I could see my princess,
looking down at my friends below,
hoping I'll live through this
last jackknife, and I can once more
be in her grasp.

—CHRIS GOUMENIS
Grade 10

That Cute Boy

That cute boy is driving me crazy,
he is so cute. He is the kind of boy
that a girl would like and worry about.
So what I'll do is just look at him
until he thinks I'm full of beauty.

—EMILY MILLER
Grade 3

Four-Leaf Clover

I can remember
when I needed you,
four leaf clover,
when my heart was in love.
I was counting on you
to give me some luck
for him to notice me.
You never came through
so my rabbit is
going to eat you!

—SUSANA QUIJANO
Grade 9

The Big Gate

My friend is a millionaire;
whenever I go there
the big gate opens.
That's why I like her.

—ROSALYN PACSON
Grade 3

Leave Me Alone

The girls leave me alone
because I told them to
leave me alone.
I go in the forest
and give crumbs to the birds,
then I try to open my lips
but they are frozen shut.

—STEPHANIE BYRNE
Grade 3

Some Day

Some day I'll show that beauty
what life is really about.
Some day I'll tear
her golden hair
right out of her fragile head.
Some day I'll see her freckled face
crying at my feet.
Some day I will have glory over her,
and I will brag
about her defeat.

—AMELIA DOYLE
Grade 5

No Secrets in the School Yard

As the wind blows,
the clouds drift overhead.
I put the collar of my heavy coat
on my neck up higher.
I can faintly hear calling birds,
and laughter fills my ears
from all directions.
A gruesome boy is teasing me,
playing with my emotions
about a certain someone.

—JENNIFER DOMINESEY
Grade 9

A Lost Friend

You're leaving me.
Please don't go so soon!
I've only begun to know you.
The flowers die in the rain of me.

—EVAN MARIE OXLEY
Grade 11

The creek is my friend
it talks with me by
falling over the rocks,
but the sun also
likes my friend
and likes to take
him in the sky

—SCOTT DENSON
Grade 7

Loving

I have a crush on a girl.
But everybody says I am
a jerk. So I am not going
to ask her out. Because she
might say I am a jerk too.
Oh, I get a chill even thinking
about her. Maybe if I send her
some flowers, she will know
how much I care. Or if
I send her some earrings
to show her how much I
think she is pretty.

—GERRY MORALES
Grade 5

Love Lost

My love
is lost
in the dark sky.
I lie in my bed
and close my eyes.
In the night
I wake up
and feel
my spirit healing.
But I still
know my energy
is
    lost
        in
            love.

—BREANNA HODGESON
Grade 4

Friends

I didn't want her
hurt by him. Then
I hurt him. He doesn't
talk to her anymore,
but he and I are
friends.

—LISA FORSYTHE
Grade 10

Debt

I feel in debt about
who I am, for I am
a little money hoarder,
as people call me,
but someone is not
going to call me this
and will be my friend.

—JOEY MANSON
Grade 7

Chasing the Light

If I were a moth
I'd fly to the light
that I see within you.
It's the only light
I know that
will never singe
my delicate wings.

—Liz Flynn
Grade 10

Girls are like swans; they
swim into minds with
open feathers.

—James Deloatch
Grade 7

My Comfort

For the thousandth time
I look in the mirror
and I see someone with beauty
Lots of people say I'm not
but who cares what
they think
I know I'm beautiful
And as long as I wake up
every day and see it
I'll be happy with myself
And each time I turn
a different age I'll wake up
with more experienced beauty!

—FALON LIPFORD
Grade 6

Who Am I?

I am like a gate
without a name.
I am like stars making something.
I wish
I could be like other children,
but I am just a dud.
I want to be
like horses that have names.

—JACOB MAYES
Grade 4

I Saw Myself

I think I am in love
For I am drawing violets.
I feel this joy within my soul.
And yesterday I saw myself in the river
And for the first time
I smiled.

—KAREN NAVAREZ
Grade 4

Mistakes

There I stood
with a bat in my hands
as a ball came toward me
like a comet,
but I just stood there
as the ball crossed the plate.
There was nothing left
but me, the wind,
and the rows of bases,
but no tears
fell from my eyes
as the boys came up
to me and said,
"It's all right. Everyone
makes mistakes."

—GRANT COOK
Grade 4

Lost and Found

She walks with sorrow in her eyes.
She has lost a loved one.
A boy walks with her,
his hair as tough as hay.
She has lost a loved one.
She has lost a loved one.
They sing and dance as if it were
the last day on earth.

—GLEN KEMP
Grade 7

The Secret Kingdom

POEMS ABOUT SOLITUDE & SPIRIT

*I am too alone in the world, and not alone
  enough
to make every minute holy. . . .
I want to be with those who know secret things
or else alone.*

—from *Selected Poems of Rainer Maria Rilke*
translated by Robert Bly

When I'm Alone

When my friends are out,
my parents gone shopping,
and the rain pouring,
I like to wander into the attic
to see,
to find,
things I've never seen,
never found,
to learn things never learned,
things never mentioned
that I have discovered myself.

—COREY BARGER
Grade 7

My Kingdom

I am a sanctuary of quietness.
My doors always stand
and my kingdom never falls.

> —SARAH WILEY
> *Grade 7*

Crazy

I would like
to be a saint.
But not talk
to the lambs.
'Cause people might
come up to me
and think I'm crazy.

> —SHELLY SMITH
> *Grade 8*

A Boat of Blue

I will hop in a boat of blue
And drive through the marsh.
The cool breeze will gently brush
    against my face.
My thoughts will be like honey
    on biscuits,
And jam on toast.
Except for the little vroom of the motor,
There will be silence.
It will be summer,
When horseflies bite your toes.
I will be king of my quiet place.

—GLENN HOFFMAN
Grade 5

The Sun Pulls the Weeds

A lonely Coke can lies forgotten
   in the grass;
the sun pulls the weeds up over its
   rusted body.
A pine tree stands nearby,
its branches like outstretched arms;
it serves as a perch for a misplaced robin,
who calls for its mate.
The breeze blows over me,
lifting my thoughts to the days ahead.

—CHRISTOPHER LENAT (1970–1991)
Grade 12

At dusk time, I love to hold
a battered football, in a lonely, overcast
stadium, and talk to God of my
mistakes.

—CAREY CASH
Grade 11

The Explorer

The traveler in me awakens
As I sleep at night
Without the burden of my body
My soul can wander
To faraway and distant places
Within myself

—TIA WITHERSPOON
Grade 9

There's a feeling inside
me that has no end.
There's a feeling inside
me that never began.

—PIA WRIGHT
Grade 8

My Thoughts

My thoughts are strange sometimes
Sometimes my thoughts make me see
spirits flying through the air
and sometimes my thoughts make me see
love going everywhere
and sometimes my thoughts make
my energy go wild
and sometimes my thoughts make
day turn into night
and sometimes my thoughts go away
and leave me all alone

—AMELIA NUTTER
Grade 3

I see not through my eyes
only through my heart and
what I see through my heart
is lovelier than any eye could see.

—SHARON BALES
Grade 8

My Quiet Place

It's dawn and I'm sitting on the dock.
Fog fills the air.
Ripples in the water splash up at me.
I have two things with me—a book and
    my thoughts.
I like this better than another TV show.

—VINCENT ROSSMEIER
Grade 4

On the Road to God

On the road to God I see a cow from
    the pasture.
There's a willow tree on the road to God.
There's a gentle shower on the road
    to God.
It feels like summer on the road to God.

—LAURA NOVELLO
Grade 3

The Long and Short Cut

One day my friend and I were
    walking home.
We got to a place where we had to
    make a decision.
Dusty thought the long cut was the
    short cut.
I thought the short cut was the short cut.
Dusty said, go this way, it has deer
    and stuff like that.
I said, my feet hurt so I'm going this way.
Dusty said, this way has pretty flowers
    for your mom.
I said, go this way and you might go
    through the place where
God forgives you everything
    you did wrong.

—BRIAN STRODE
Grade 5

Forgiveness makes
you feel like you
did the right thing
anyway.

—CHRISTI MORRIS
Grade 4

If I had thrown salt over my shoulder
I could not have been luckier
than to walk in the white silence
    of the snow.

—LISA CARDONE SESSONS
Grade 11

Every day I think about
the god and the weeds
outside and sometimes
I hold my doll.

—TRACY BISHOP
Grade 4

The swings at nighttime
are quiet
and asleep
as if someone great
laid a blanket over them.

—JOSEPH CAUTHEN III
Grade 5

The bones of God could be made
    of crushed stars,
Shimmering, twinkling stars, crushed
    into a priceless powder,
Powder that runs through your fingers
    with the sound of silver bells.

—CARA CANNON
Grade 10

Me, Who Am I

I am alone in the woods.
I am not a bookworm.
I am on the moss in my dream.

My soul is drawing a giant with crayons.
The giant is a small child.
Its soul is drawing a picture of me.

The master is not truthful.
He pretends he works.
He does it for gold.
I don't like it.

I am forgetful.
I make mistakes.
Who am I?
I black out in the grass.

—MEAGAN THOMPSON
Grade 4

Life and Me

Life is a mystery of hard
feelings and choices; it looks
like it will never end; the sky is blue
and the water is crystal-like; it is
   like looking
through a glass where you can see but
   not understand.
When the wind blows on my face I feel
   like my soul is
that wind, and all my troubles blow
   away with it.
In the night I feel angels coming and
   caring for me
in the moonlight. I feel like my fingers
   are touching
God's fingers and when this happens I
   feel I am an

angel myself. Not a snake or a lion can
   have this feeling
but I can. It feels so wonderful; the
   motion of my body
is so great that tears come to my eyes
   and I ask
myself what is this feeling? I feel my
   soul transforming
into a spirit of fire and at the end
   of this feeling
there is triumph and a beautiful dream.

—JOSÉ MACATO
Grade 7

Index of Poets

Acknowledgments

This book is the result of the interest and efforts of many people who care about children and hold the vision of giving voice to their expression through the arts. My special thanks to Philip Graham, who first encouraged me to work with children; Helen Waid, of the Virginia Beach city schools, who taught me in my first uncertain steps in the classroom; Nancy Morgan, for inspiring me through the depth of her commitment to bringing the arts and children together; Lynn Silverstein, for her genius and generosity in assisting artists like myself in crafting workshops of excellence for teachers; Michael and Brook Thompson, Steve and Cindy Halliday, Mary and Ted Colwell, and Chantal Andrews, for opening their homes to me during extended residencies in various schools; Betty Smith, Mary Ann Mullany, Donna Moore, Alex Marshall, and the *Virginia Pilot and Star Ledger* newspaper, for their generous help in locating missing students for this anthology; the John F. Kennedy Center for the Performing Arts' Education Programs, for providing me with an ever-wider forum for developing and presenting my work to teachers; and to the Virginia Commission on the Arts, which provided grants to several schools in which I held workshops.

My thanks to my sister, Jayn Zopf, and to John C. Carr, for reading the manuscript and for their helpful suggestions. My deepest thanks of all to my wife, Patricia, who—through some very difficult times—never wavered in her loving support of my decision to go work with the children.